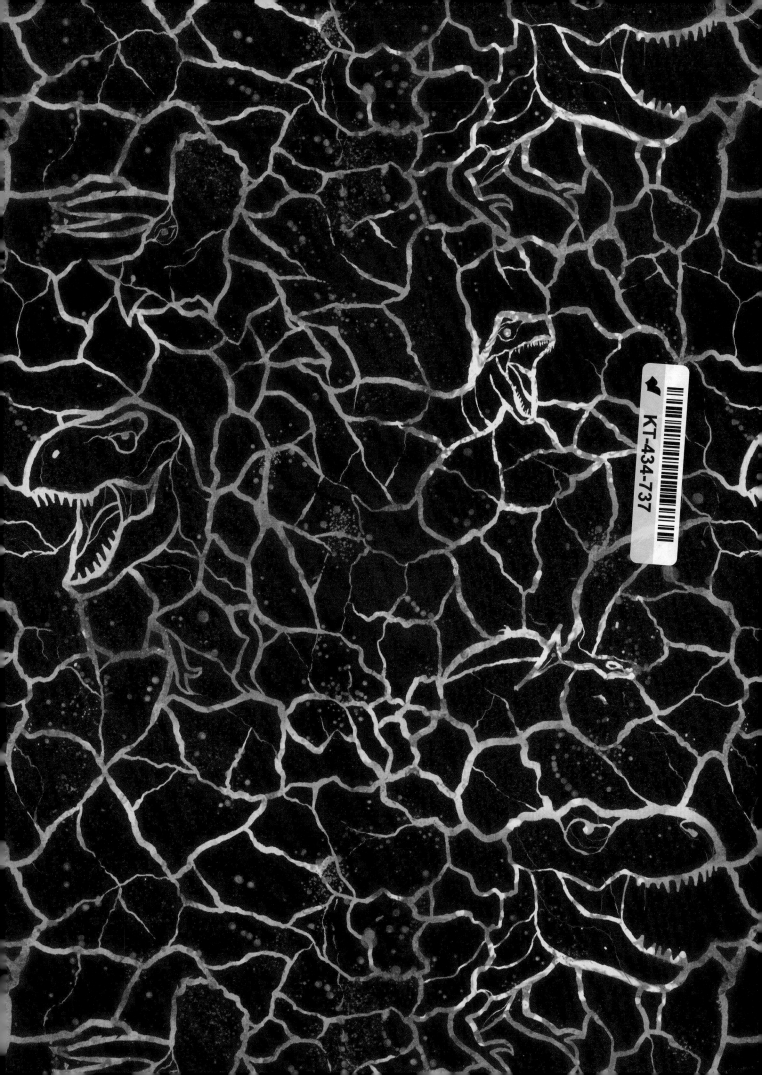

EGMONT
We bring stories to life

First published in Great Britain 2018 by Egmont UK Limited
The Yellow Building, 1 Nicholas Road, London W11 4AN

Written by Joshua Winning and Katrina Pallant
Designed by Maddox Philpot, Ian Pollard and Ant Duke

UNIVERSAL®
A COMCAST COMPANY

ISBN 978 1 4052 9116 3
68620/1
Printed in Italy

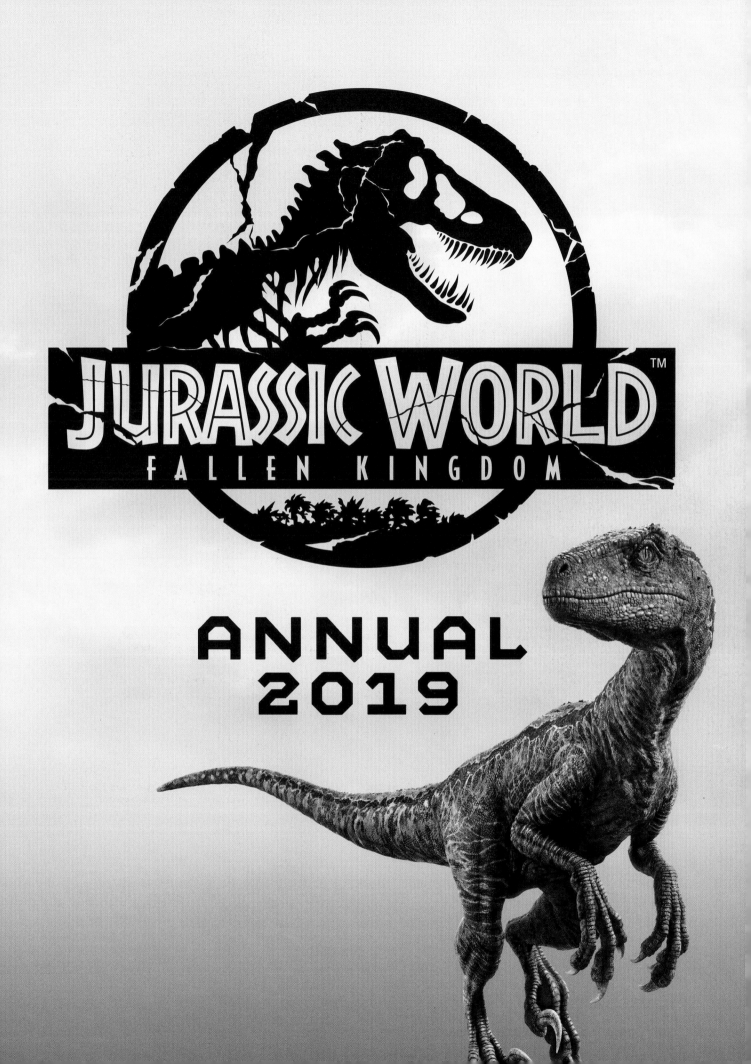

JURASSIC WORLD™
FALLEN KINGDOM

ANNUAL 2019

CONTENTS

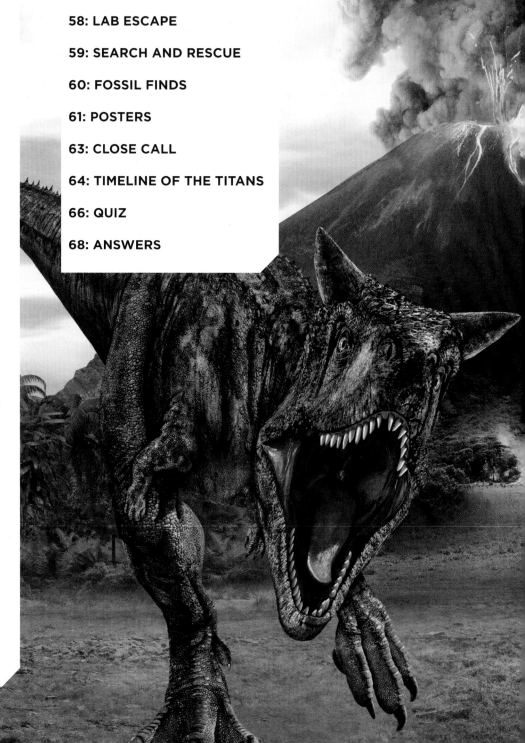

Welcome back to Jurassic World! Time to track some Raptors, avoid some lava, defeat some villains and have another amazing adventure with the dinosaurs of Isla Nublar. Fill in your stats here.

NAME:

AGE:

FAVOURITE DINOSAUR:

SPECIAL SKILL:

Years after the incident at Jurassic World, the park lay abandoned in a sad state of disrepair. Overhead a helicopter watched as a submarine entered the lagoon. The two men inside the sub had orders to retrieve an important sunken object.

'There she is,' the pilot said, as the sub's floodlights illuminated the bones of the *Indominus rex*. One of the crew operated the sub's robotic arms, grabbing a piece of bone. 'Air One, specimen collected,' the pilot radioed to the helicopter. 'Sending to surface.' As the specimen floated to the surface, a huge shadow passed behind the sub and her unsuspecting crew.

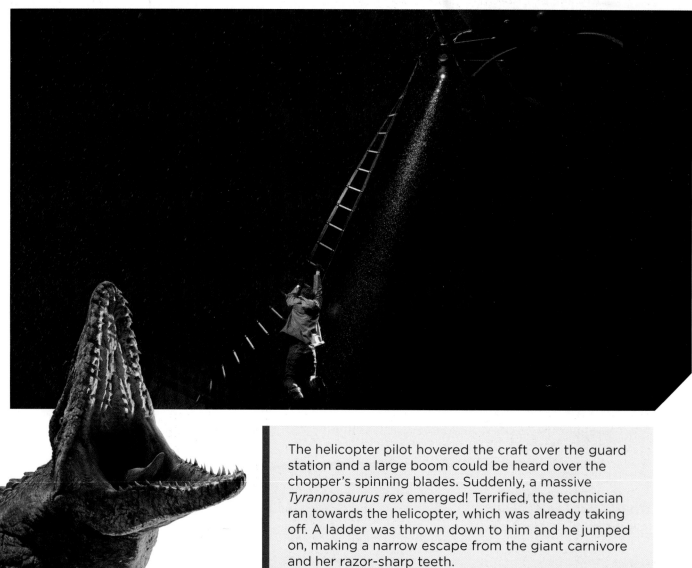

The helicopter pilot hovered the craft over the guard station and a large boom could be heard over the chopper's spinning blades. Suddenly, a massive *Tyrannosaurus rex* emerged! Terrified, the technician ran towards the helicopter, which was already taking off. A ladder was thrown down to him and he jumped on, making a narrow escape from the giant carnivore and her razor-sharp teeth.

The technician breathed a sigh of relief. But then a *Mosasaurus* roared up out of the lagoon and engulfed the screaming technician! The helicopter flew away over the mountains.

Three years later, the revelation of an active volcano on Isla Nublar was reported on the news. 'Isla Nublar now faces a new threat. Geologists predict an extinction-level event will soon kill off the last dinosaurs known to exist on the planet.'

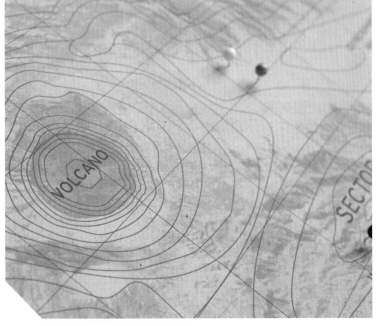

This raised a debate in the Senate about whether the dinosaurs should be saved, or if they should be left to become extinct again. Dr Ian Malcolm was invited to give his thoughts. 'How many times do you have to see the evidence?' he said, adding that he thought things had gone too far and humanity could be on the verge of extinction. Malcolm had first-hand experience of the chaos and destruction caused by Jurassic Park and the original cloned dinosaurs. He believed that the course of natural history had been altered and the volcano was 'a necessary correction.'

On the other side of the argument was the Dinosaur Protection Group, run by its founder and former Jurassic World Operations Manager Claire Dearing. The Group was leading the fight to save the dinosaurs, fundraising and campaigning in order to encourage the government to launch a rescue mission to Isla Nublar.

Her colleagues Zia Rodriguez, a paleoveterinarian, and Franklin Webb, the Group's resident computer expert, were both working hard to make a difference. After the Senate committee made its announcement that they would not recommend any action be taken to save the dinosaurs, everyone was downhearted. 'They're all going to die,' Claire said, 'and no one cares.'

'We do,' Franklin insisted. Just then, Claire received a phone call with exciting news.

Claire had been invited to the Lockwood Estate, a mansion hidden in a forest of redwood trees in northern California. The estate was owned by the old partner of John Hammond, the founder of Jurassic Park. Claire was greeted by Eli Mills, who ran Lockwood's foundation, and led into the library. The glass cases on the far side of the room held elaborate dioramas of dinosaurs fighting, feeding, and caring for their young. There was even a massive *Triceratops* skull in the middle of the room.

Mills gestured to a model of a mountainous island in the sea. 'We have a piece of land,' he explained. 'A sanctuary our environmentalists say will support all the species currently on Isla Nublar.'

At that moment Sir Benjamin Lockwood emerged in a wheelchair. The old man did not seem in good health. 'This was John Hammond's dream, you know,' he said. 'No fences, no cages, no tourists.'

Claire thought it was wonderful. 'What do you need from me?' she asked.

DINOSAUR RESCUE

Meet the humans on a mission to save dinosaurs from another extinction.

CLAIRE DEARING

'An entire generation has grown up in a world where dinosaurs exist. And now they'll have to watch them go extinct.'

Claire was Operations manager at the Jurassic World theme park, until the dinosaurs broke loose! After surviving an encounter with the *Indominus rex*, she has decided that dinosaurs need our help. Now leading the Dinosaur Protection Group, an organisation she founded, Claire embarks on an operation to rescue the dinosaurs before it's too late.

OWEN GRADY

'I rode a motorcycle through the jungle with a pack of Raptors.'

Owen is a dinosaur trainer who was employed at Jurassic World and witnessed the incident that shut down the park. Owen has retired from training Raptors to live a quieter life, and is reluctant to join Claire. But when he learns that Blue, a *Velociraptor* he raised from birth, is still alive, he joins the mission to save the dinosaurs on Isla Nublar.

BENJAMIN LOCKWOOD

'*This was John Hammond's dream.*'

An old friend of John Hammond, the creator of Jurassic Park, Benjamin was a financial backer as John developed the idea for the dinosaur clones. Now, Benjamin wants to set up his very own dinosaur sanctuary at the Lockwood Estate, but he needs Claire and Owen's help transporting the dinosaurs from Isla Nublar.

IAN MALCOLM

'*Life cannot be contained.*'

Dr Ian Malcolm is an expert in chaos theory, and after surviving an encounter with the dinosaurs at Jurassic Park he has a few things to say about the restoration of these species. He believes that the volcano is nature's way of correcting the mistake made by bringing these prehistoric animals back from extinction.

FRANKLIN WEBB

'*Nature's angry.*'

A member of the Dinosaur Protection Group, Franklin uses social media to help spread the word about dinosaur welfare. The resident computer expert is brought to Isla Nublar to help get the old tracking system back online.

ZIA RODRIGUEZ

'*Without me, you'll never get her back to camp alive.*'

Zia is a paleoveterinarian – a vet for dinosaurs! As part of the Dinosaur Protection Group, it's her job to ensure Blue makes it off Isla Nublar alive after she is injured.

SAVE THE DINOSAURS!

Create your own campaign poster for the Dinosaur Protection Group.

WE MADE THEM, WE SAVE THEM!

THEY WERE HERE FIRST!

DINOSAURS HAVE RIGHTS TOO!

SAVE OUR SAURS!

NATURE'S GIANTS MUST LIVE!

Put the picture back together in the right order to recreate the *Indominus rex*.

1 2
3 4
5 6

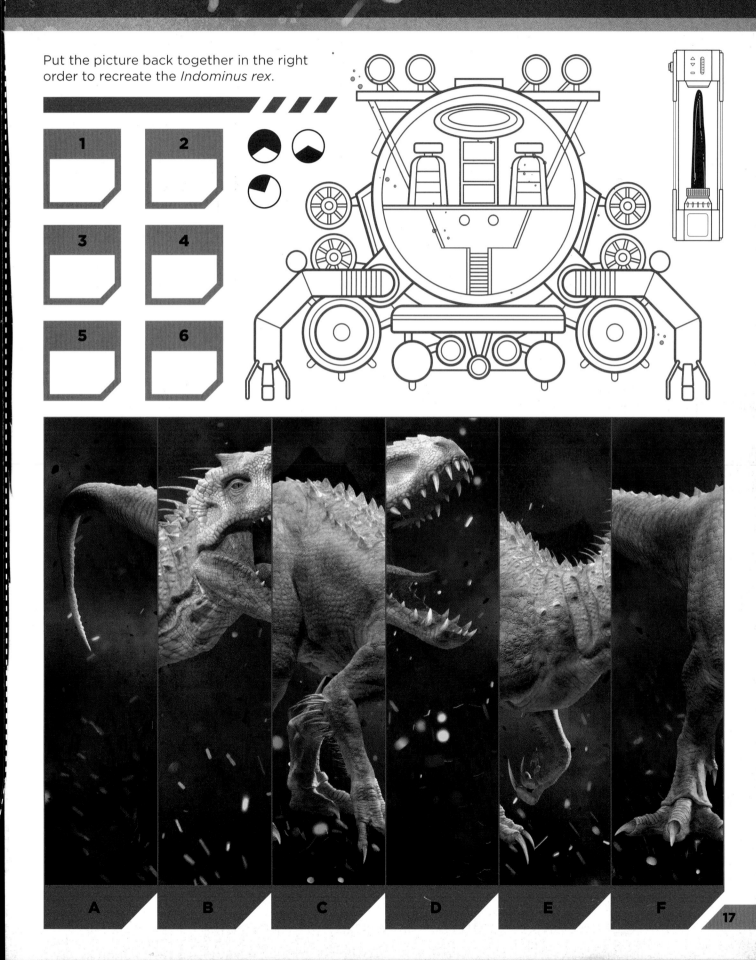

A   B   C   D   E   F

POD PROBLEM

Gyrospheres were a great way to get around Jurassic World, but now they are all in ruins. Rearrange the squares to rebuild your Gyrosphere so that it looks like the one on the right.

ISLA NUBLAR

Home to the dinosaurs of Jurassic World, this little island in the Pacific Ocean is an exotic paradise – as long as you stay out of the way of stampeding dinosaurs!

Parks:
Jurassic Park, never opened
Jurassic World, active 2005-2015

Name meaning: Clouded Island
Location: 120 miles from Costa Rica
Size: 22 square miles
Discovered by: Diego Fernandez in 1525

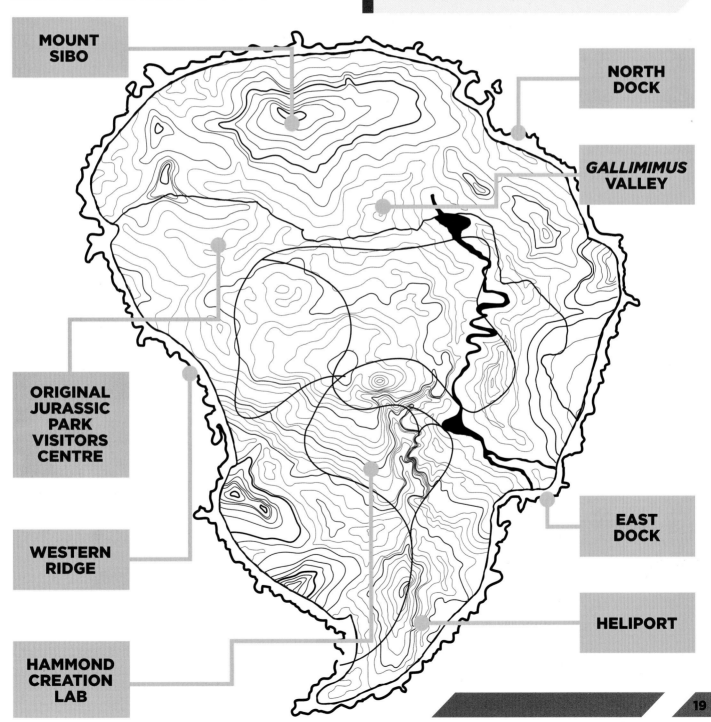

MOUNT SIBO

NORTH DOCK

GALLIMIMUS VALLEY

ORIGINAL JURASSIC PARK VISITORS CENTRE

WESTERN RIDGE

EAST DOCK

HELIPORT

HAMMOND CREATION LAB

Lockwood needed Claire to travel to the island in order to locate a tracking system that only her handprint could activate. They also needed help with a particular dinosaur, a *Velociraptor* named Blue. They knew there was only one man who could help.

Claire went to see Owen high in the Sierra Nevada mountains, where he was building himself a cabin next to a lake, miles away from the nearest town. After the events at Jurassic World, Claire knew Owen would not want to help. He had spent years training the *Velociraptors*, including raising Blue from a baby. But he would not be easily convinced to join this ill-advised rescue mission. 'When these animals are gone, that's it! There's no more,' she cried. But he did not budge.

That evening, Owen sat alone in his trailer in front of an old laptop, face aglow from flickering video images of memories past. On his screen Owen watched a video from several years ago of him training Baby Blue. He smiled to himself for a moment, remembering how it felt to be there more than three years ago, and realised that he had no choice. If Blue was in danger, Owen had to save her.

The plane reached Isla Nublar.

After several hours in the air, the plane reached Isla Nublar. Claire and Owen gazed through the windows down at the abandoned island as the plane circled it. Smoke rose from the volcano. They could see the old Aviary where the *Pteranodons* once lived. It was now so covered in vines it was barely recognisable. They caught each other's eyes, remembering the carnage they'd seen on this island.

The plane was met by a heavily-armed man named Wheatley. He and his men had set up a basecamp guarded by armoured vehicles and they all carried tranquiliser guns. Wheatley briefed the new arrivals on the state of the volcano. 'Our volcanologist says it could happen anytime now, the tremors are getting more frequent.' He also told them that he had lost five men already to the inhabitants of the island, specifically Blue.

The group set off in a military vehicle through the jungle towards the bunker that housed the tracking system. Ash fell from the smoking volcano looming in the distance. They passed through Main Street and onto Gyrosphere Valley. The vehicles rolled through the overgrown meadow littered with the bleached bones of dinosaurs that carnivores had picked clean.

Eventually they arrived at a bunker dug into the mountain. It was dusty and full of long-dead computers and radio equipment. Claire put her palm against a hand scanner. It lit up, authorising entry to the system. Franklin patched his laptop into the system and quickly pulled up a map of the park with dots showing each dinosaur's location. 'Can you single out the Raptor?' Wheatley said. Franklin typed in a code revealing Blue's location. He made the tracking system portable so Owen took a tablet and set off to find his old friend.

In the jungle, Owen got out of the military vehicle to track Blue on foot. Wheatley and his men brought up the rear with their tranquiliser rifles at the ready. Owen worried that Blue wouldn't recognise him and might try to attack him. He turned and was confronted with the *Velociraptor!*

The Raptor hissed and snapped, showing her sharp teeth. Owen offered her a dead rat. She sniffed the air and growled. As she opened her mouth to take the rat she was shot with a tranquiliser dart! 'No!' yelled Owen, before he too was felled by a dart. Blue was loaded into a cage and Owen was left unconscious on the ground. The volcano began to erupt around him.

Meanwhile, in the bunker, Claire and Franklin realised they had been trapped by Wheatley's men. The volcano tremors were getting worse by the minute. Another booming sound echoed down the corridor and a proximity alarm sounded. An animal with an embedded tracking device appeared to be moving through the maze of underground tunnels towards the bunker.

Suddenly, a *Baryonyx* emerged!
The carnivore stalked them, backing them up against a wall.

Before the *Baryonyx* could do any damage with her crocodile-like teeth, a wall of lava poured down between her and them. It seemed there was no escape. Then, Claire noticed a ladder leading up to a hatch and the pair rushed to clamber up. Feeling the hot breath of the *Baryonyx* rushing up from below, they emerged into the sunlight and clanged the hatch shut on the *Baryonyx*. They found themselves standing in Gyrosphere Valley watching Owen run towards them...

Together, Claire, Owen and Franklin sprinted for the ocean cliff, the only way off the island. Claire and Franklin jumped into a Gyrosphere, but before Owen could climb in with them, he was attacked by a *Carnotaurus*. The nightmarish carnivore stalked Owen around the Gyrosphere knocking the glass ball with her tail. Claire and Franklin began plummeting downhill.

The *Carnotaurus* turned her attention back to Owen, but then a *T. rex* snatched the *Carnotaurus* in her jaws and tossed the dinosaur aside like a rag doll. The volcano exploded behind him as Owen ran after the Gyrosphere, but as a cloud of black ash swallowed him, he watched in terror as the Gyrosphere rocketed off the cliff-edge into the ocean.

As water started to flood into the Gyrosphere, Claire and Franklin desperately tried to open the door, but it wouldn't budge. Dinosaurs crashed into the water around them, thrashing their huge limbs as they sank beneath the waves. Owen dove in and began to wrestle with the door. Claire and Franklin became completely submerged as Owen finally managed to pull the door aside. They swam to the surface, avoiding the flailing creatures around them, emerging on the beach spluttering and panting for breath.

As the group recovered, they saw Wheatley's men loading lots of unconscious dinosaurs onto a ship. 'We need to get on that boat,' Owen said. Glowing, red lava began to spill over the side of the cliff above and they knew they didn't have much time. Owen, Claire and Franklin jumped into a forgotten truck and sped up the ramp onto the ship. The crew members were too busy watching the island burn behind them to notice the stowaways.

BLUE

Blue, the biggest and cleverest of her pack, is the last *Velociraptor* on Isla Nublar. She is cunning, quick and lethal. She will not be easy to track or capture.

VELOCIRAPTOR

Name meaning: Swift Thief
Period: Early Cretaceous
Discovered: China
Diet: Carnivorous
Length: 3.3m
Weight: 60kg

FUN FACT

An adult *Velociraptor* can bite with a force of over 8,000 Newtons, or equivalent to a large American alligator.

TRACKING TIP

When training her as an infant, Owen noticed that Blue started to display signs of compassion towards him. The only way to catch Blue is by bringing along Owen.

BLUE OF A KIND

Tracking Blue is not an easy task, especially when you're seeing double! Can you find two identical *Velociraptors* below?

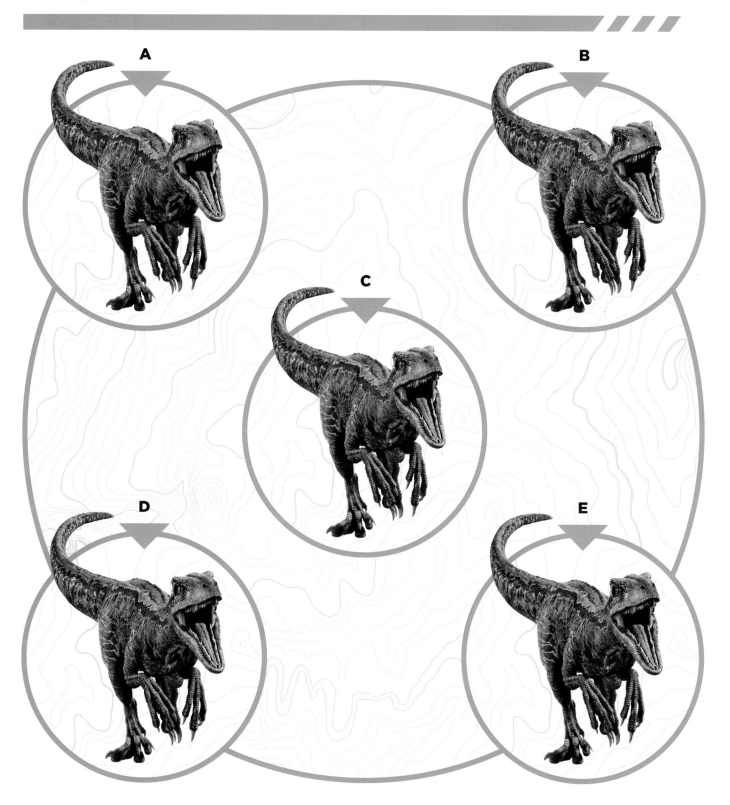

T. REX

The *T. rex* is arguably the most famous dinosaur of them all. When the park was open, the *T. rex* Kingdom attraction drew massive crowds due to its inhabitant's incredible size and fearsome roar.

T. REX

Name meaning: King Tyrant Lizard
Period: Late Cretaceous
Discovered: Western North America
Diet: Carnivorous
Length: 13.5m
Weight: 8,400kg

FUN FACT

An adult *Tyrannosaurus* requires at least 140kg of meat every day. Thanks to extra powerful neck muscles, the *T. rex* can throw up to 50kg of meat into the air and catch it in her mouth.

TRACKING TIP

Dr Wu's clone is extremely sensitive to scents and is known to hunt prey by honing in on its movement. Approach with extreme caution and don't make any sudden movements.

PREHISTORIC PUZZLE

The *T. rex* is on the run from the erupting volcano. Complete the scene by finding the right puzzle pieces to fill the gaps.

The *T. rex's* bite force is over 3,500 kg of pressure - over ten times that of an adult alligator!

BARYONYX

When Jurassic World opened, these crocodile-like dinosaurs became the stars of the Cretaceous Cruise on the north-eastern side of Isla Nublar. Beware the sly *Baryonyx*, who loves to take its prey by surprise!

BARYONYX

Name meaning: Heavy Claw
Period: Early Cretaceous
Discovered: England/Spain
Diet: Carnivorous
Length: 9.3m
Weight: 1,700kg

FUN FACT

The *Baryonyx* doesn't just look like a crocodile. Much like her cousins, this dinosaur claps her jaws and splashes in the water to communicate.

TRACKING TIP

The *Baryonyx* can't get enough of fish. If you want to locate a *Baryonyx*, a river would be a good place to look. They just love going fishing.

HIDDEN LAVA

Claire and Franklin must escape the *Baryonyx* by avoiding the lava. Some of the empty squares in the grid below conceal lava, and the numbers tell you how many of their adjacent squares – including diagonally adjacent squares – contain lava. None of the numbered squares have lava in them. Can you find all of the lava and save the day?

PTERANODON

The biggest flying reptile in the park by far, the *Pteranodon* has a massive wingspan of up to 20 feet, which is larger than any known bird. They are moderately aggressive and fast during flight.

PTERANODON

Name meaning: Toothless Wing
Period: Late Cretaceous
Discovered: North America
Diet: Carnivorous
Length: 2.5m
Weight: 3kg

FUN FACT

Pteranodons sound akin to modern day seagulls, communicating with each other in screeches and squawks. They also roost together in groups, often near cliffsides.

TRACKING TIP

Keeping well out of sight is the best way to make sure you don't upset a *Pteranodon* – if she spots you, she will react very aggressively and may even make you her next target.

PTERANODON ATTACK!

The *Pteranodon* are built for speed – and they're looking for their next meal. Can you find them all in this picture before it's too late?

WHAT IS A CARNIVORE?

A carnivore is a creature that survives by eating other animals. Around 35% of dinosaurs were meat-eaters and they had an important job in the world's ecosystem – by eating other animals, they kept the population stable. Carnivores had sharp teeth and strong jaws to devour their prey, and their long, muscular legs helped them catch their next meal.

The *Carnotaurus* is a very large dinosaur, with distinctive horns, which are not weapons, but social displays the dinosaurs use to identify each other. The *Mosasaurus* is a water dinosaur that's almost as big as a blue whale! She lived in the Jurassic World Lagoon, a 3 million gallon pool where she would thrust her enormous, tooth-lined jaws up out of the water during the popular *Mosasaurus* Feeding Show.

CARNOTAURUS

Name meaning: Meat-Eating Bull
Period: Late Cretaceous
Discovered: Argentina
Diet: Carnivorous
Length: 10.4m
Weight: 2,100kg

The *Carnotaurus* will typically eat very quickly so the *T. rex*, an opportunistic hunter, will not arrive and take over the carcass.

MOSASAURUS

Name meaning: Meuse River Lizard
Period: Late Cretaceous
Discovered: France
Diet: Carnivorous
Length: 25.9m
Weight: 29,000kg

The *Mosasaurus* has a second set of teeth on her upper jaw to stop any captured prey from escaping her mouth.

CARNIVORE CREW

Wild carnivores on Isla Nublar have their pick of the prey, but also have to watch out for each other. Spot five differences between these two pictures of the meat-eating creatures.

WHAT IS A HERBIVORE?

A herbivore is a creature that only eats plants and vegetables. Plant-eating dinosaurs usually had blunt teeth for chewing and stripping greenery – and some even had cheek pouches for storing their food! Herbivores are often eaten by carnivores, putting them lower down the food chain.

APATOSAURUS

Name meaning: Deceptive Lizard
Period: Late Jurassic
Discovered: North America
Diet: Herbivorous
Length: 22m
Weight: 20,000kg

The long tail of the *Apatosaurus* isn't just for show. These dinosaurs can crack the whip-like ends of their tails to make a loud sound, which will ward off any threats.

TRICERATOPS

Name meaning: Three-Horned Face
Period: Late Cretaceous
Discovered: North America
Diet: Herbivorous
Length: 8m
Weight: 10,000kg

Despite being a herbivore, the *Triceratops* is an aggressive animal. Fossils show evidence that these dinosaurs frequently locked horns with members of their own species in combat.

HERBIVORE HERD

Find the dinosaur that appears only once in this grid of herbivores. It is actually an omnivore – a dinosaur that can live solely on vegetation, but has also been known to eat small animals.

DINOSAUR DASH

Now that you have tracked all the dinosaurs, help them escape the volcano by loading them on to the ship!

START

A *Pteranodon* avoids hitting you. Move forward 1 space.

Your pulley breaks when loading the *T. rex* – move back 2 spaces.

You lose track of Blue again – miss a go.

You and a friend take it in turn to roll a dice and navigate around the board following the instructions that you land on.

A path of lava blocks your way – go back to the start.

The *Carnotaurus* has you in her sights. Miss a go.

You find the missing *Triceratops* – move forward 2 spaces.

FINISH

Back at Lockwood's mansion, Mills met with a serious-looking man in a business suit. 'Mr. Eversoll,' he said, 'so nice to meet you in person after all this time.' Eversoll was an agent who Mills hoped would help with lining up buyers for the many dinosaurs returning from Isla Nublar.

Wheatley's crew worked for Mills, not Lockwood! Mills had ulterior motives in rescuing the dinosaurs, and wanted to show Eversoll what he had in mind. It did not involve a sanctuary, but something much more sinister. Eversoll did not think the propsal was worth his time. 'No, wait,' Mills said urgently. 'Let me show you something.'

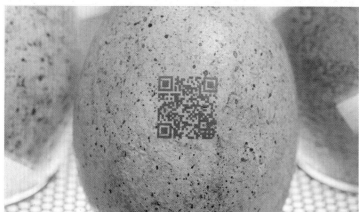

Mills led him to an elevator and punched a code into a control pad. 'The sale of the Isla Nublar dinosaurs is to finance our future operations,' Mills explained. 'It's seed money. Just the prelude to something much more ambitious.'

Both men were unaware that Lockwood's granddaughter Maisie was watching. The little girl ran to tell her grandfather what his trusted advisor was really up to.

'If our history has taught us anything,' Mills said, 'it's that man is inevitably drawn to war. And that he'll use any means to win.'

'You're going to weaponise the dinosaurs?' asked Eversoll.

Mills showed Eversoll a hologram of the *Indominus rex*, revealing that a vicious new dinosaur had been created using its DNA. 'We call it the *Indoraptor* in honour of its illustrious heritage,' said Mills proudly.

'Show it to me,' said Eversoll, as his eyes lit up.

Mills led Eversoll down a metal spiral staircase. The lower level was full of steel cages built into cement walls. Through the bars, Eversoll could make out a shadowy animal in the dark cage. It was ten feet tall and sleek. He could hear it breathing quietly.

'Oh, I wouldn't stand there,' Mills warned Eversoll. He looked down and saw that his feet were on a line of red tape. He quickly took a step back.

'We need to show this thing to the buyers,' Eversoll said, excited. The *Indoraptor* growled.

The next day, Maisie followed Mills to the underground cells. Snuffling sounds came from within the cages and Maisie crept closer. She gasped in fear as a long, clawed arm stretched for her through the bars. It was the *Indoraptor!*

Something grabbed Maisie's arm and she screamed, but it wasn't the *Indoraptor*, it was Mills. Angrily, he hauled her off to her room and locked her in.

In his bed, Lockwood reprimanded Mills after discovering from Maisie that he wanted to sell the dinosaurs off to the highest bidder. 'Did you think you would get away with it? In my own house?' he cried. But Mills didn't want to hear it, and sabotaged Lockwood's IV drip, turning it up to a dangerous level and leaving him to die.

Meanwhile, Wheatley's cargo ship docked and Franklin was mistaken for a member of the dock crew. Miserably, he was forced to go and help the crew unload the dinosaur cages. Helplessly, Owen and Claire watched as all the trucks – including the one carrying Zia and Blue – revved off the ship towards the thick forest surrounding Lockwood's Estate.

At the entrance gate, Claire and Owen sat in the truck they had stolen from the cargo ship and watched as the dinosaurs were brought into a massive basement under Lockwood's mansion. Wheatley spotted them and apprehended them and threw them in a cage too.

They received a visit from Mills, who apologised for lying to Claire about his true intentions for the Isla Nublar dinosaurs, but Claire was so angry she tried to fight him through the bars.

'You betrayed a dying man! For money!' she said, landing a punch to his mouth.

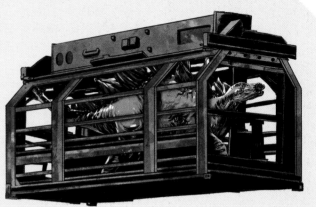

Mills left to meet the buyers for the auction. Eversoll had lined up pharmaceutical giants, arms dealers and oil magnates, anyone with deep pockets and questionable values, to bid on the dinosaurs.

Owen peeked through a tiny window and discovered there was a *Stygimoloch* in the cell next to them. The herbivore had a dome-shaped skull that could be up to nine inches thick. 'Well, look who just woke up!' he said, and smiled at Claire. 'We're getting out of here.' He gave a sharp whistle, which irritated Stiggy, who turned to ram the wall between their cells. She crashed through into their cell and through the cell door, running off down the hall.

Claire and Owen hurried out of their cell, finding Maisie scared after her last encounter with Mills. She recognised Owen from the videos she had watched, and decided to trust him.

A weaponised dinosaur created for use in combat, the *Indoraptor* is a top-secret new hybrid that few people have ever seen. Unlike the attraction dinosaurs of Jurassic World, the *Indoraptor* was created by a rogue faction using a DNA sample taken from the *Indominus rex* and will be auctioned off to the highest bidder.

With its streamlined body and razor-sharp teeth, the *Indoraptor* is a deadly hybrid that is cruel and almost unstoppable. Here are some clues about the scary new dinosaur from classified case files...

WARNING:

DO NOT APPROACH

Location: Unknown
Diet: Carnivorous
Hybrid characteristics: The *Indoraptor* is fast with a superior intelligence comparable to the *Velociraptor*.
Bio specs: Echo-location, heightened sense of smell.
Training: Responds to a laser
Abilities: Can isolate and track prey in complex environments. Highly adaptable to urban areas and close-quarter combat scenarios.

With the help of Dr Wu, you can create your very own dinosaur! Will it have sharp teeth, horns or a long tail? Use these dinosaurs below as inspiration for your masterpiece.

There's a fast and deadly dinosaur on your tail! The *Indoraptor* is clever and quick – colour in this terrifying hybrid and watch out for those teeth!

COLOSSAL COLOURING

Grab some pencils or pens and add a bit of colour to these Jurassic favourites.

In the garage, the auction was bringing in millions of dollars. Eversoll and Mills were thrilled. A *Stegosaurus* went for twenty-one million dollars. Just above, Owen and Claire pressed their way through a tight service tunnel full of pipes and electrical conduits, followed by Maisie. They could hear Eversoll's voice. Following the sound of it, they found a grate in the wall. Through the grate, they could see everything going on in the garage below them.

Eversoll was saying, 'And now, a special treat for the truly discriminating buyer! We'd like to preview a new asset we have been developing. We call it . . . the *Indoraptor*.' An elevator rose from the level of the containment cells up to the garage. The bidders saw the silhouette of the powerful *Indoraptor* and gasped.

'What is that thing?' Claire asked.

'The *Indoraptor* has been trained to respond to a pulse-coded laser targeting system,' Eversoll continued, 'allowing it to isolate and track prey in complex environments . . .'
A guard raised his rifle and flipped on its targeting laser. He focused the beam of light on Anton, the Russian mobster. In the cage, the *Indoraptor* responded immediately, coiling and focusing intently on the Russian.

Watching from above, Owen felt disgusted. He had to do something. He crept out into the hall. He heard a SMASH! and saw that Stiggy had made her way upstairs. He led her to the elevator and pressed the button. The bidding for the *Indoraptor* had reached thirty-two million dollars and was still rising. The *Indoraptor* roared and lunged, testing the cage bars that held it.

Suddenly, the elevator arrived and out burst Stiggy. The frantic buyers scattered as Stiggy smashed through them like bowling pins. The garage was a scene of chaos as buyers and chairs flew through the air, bashed by Stiggy. From its cage, the *Indoraptor* watched, huffing. It was hungry. Outside, by the loading dock, buyers scrambled to escape with their dinosaurs, driving off in trucks. Stiggy crashed out and raced into the forest, free.

BREACH: STORY PART 4

From inside the garage, the *Indoraptor* roared. Wheatley saw an opportunity, and headed inside. Wheatley approached the *Indoraptor* cage and shot a dart into its neck. Then he shot another, until the *Indoraptor* had fallen unconscious. Then Wheatley opened the cage and attempted to remove one of its teeth with his pliers as a trophy, but the *Indoraptor* wasn't unconscious at all, and he bit Wheatley so hard he wouldn't be pulling teeth ever again.

Now free, the *Indoraptor* worked his way through the room, looking for prey. Owen rejoined Claire and Maisie. 'Okay,' he said soothingly. 'Look at me. Stay close to me, okay? I'm gonna go first.' He led them down a narrow tunnel to escape, but they ran straight into a guard, who ordered them to halt. Just as Owen was sliding his gun over to the guard, the *Indoraptor* appeared. It slammed into the guard like a freight train. Maisie screamed and they all ran.

The *Indoraptor* came roaring around the corner. Owen slammed the door, but the *Indoraptor* crashed against it, snapping his jaws. Pushing together, Owen and Claire managed to close the door and turn the lock.

In the sub-basement lab, Dr Wu observed as samples from the *Indominus rex* were packaged up by other employees – including Franklin. While Wu was distracted talking to Zia, Franklin plunged a tranquiliser needle into his neck.

Quickly, Franklin freed Zia and they watched as Blue broke out of her cage and killed a guard. But, before the guard died, he shot at Blue, striking a nitrogen tank. The tank exploded in a fiery blaze, which Franklin and Zia narrowly escaped.

Meanwhile, the *Indoraptor* stalked Owen, Claire and Maisie through the library. The dinosaur launched itself at them, and they became separated. Maisie used the dumbwaiter to escape and the *Indoraptor* followed. Breathlessly, Owen found a guard's gun and went after them.

Owen flung open the door to Maisie's bedroom where she was cornered by the *Indoraptor*. Owen fired at the hybrid but he soon ran out of bullets. Suddenly, Blue appeared in the doorway! Seeing Owen in danger, Blue attacked the *Indoraptor*.

The two dinosaurs fought each other while Owen and Maisie made a run for it out of the window and onto the balcony. The *Indoraptor* managed to shake off Blue and followed the pair onto a glass roof. Just as the *Indoraptor* was about to reach them, Claire appeared. She pointed a rifle's laser on the roof and the dinosaur ran right at it. The glass roof broke beneath it, but it was able to hang on and began to pull itself back up. Blue jumped down from a nearby chimney and flung herself at the *Indoraptor*. The hybrid plummeted into the library below, landing right on the horns of the *Triceratops* skull.

Franklin and Zia, who had seen the whole thing, had another problem. They led Claire and Owen into the lab, where the explosion had unleashed a deadly gas. The dinosaurs still caged were choking. Owen picked Maisie up and held her. He turned her away from the awful sight of the dying dinosaurs.

Claire studied a control board, swiping through a touch screen. She found the command she was looking for. 'We can open the cell doors from here.' But this was not an easy decision to make. To release the dinosaurs into the world was a reckless, dangerous act – probably criminal. But to just stand there and watch them die, roaring and coughing, seemed inhuman.

But Maisie made the decision for them. She pressed the button, opening the doors. The dinosaurs scrambled out into the grounds. They were free.

At the loading dock, Mills attempted to salvage the Indominus bone, but a dinosaur stampede came out of nowhere as the dinosaurs fled the mansion. A *Pteranodon* swept down and plucked up one of the guards, while rampaging dinosaurs sideswiped Mills' van, sending it flying. Then, suddenly, the *T. rex* appeared and chewed Mills up! The dinosaur's huge foot smashed the glass case containing the Indominus bone into a thousand pieces.

Meanwhile, Owen, Claire, Franklin, Zia and Maisie left the mansion through the front door. Blue stood right in front of them, but Owen wasn't scared. 'She won't hurt us,' he reassured Maisie, and Blue considered the group for a moment before racing off into the woods to freedom. The group realised the world had changed forever. Now the dinosaurs roamed freely and they could be anywhere. Whose world was it now?

LAB ESCAPE

Claire and Owen are being chased by the *Indoraptor* and need to get out of the lab. Help them escape by following the pattern through the maze, moving up, down, left and right.

START

FINISH

SEARCH AND RESCUE

Now you're an expert, find the names of the Jurassic World dinosaurs in the grid below, looking forwards, backwards, up, down and diagonally.

```
S  S  R  R  B  B  S  S  J  A  T  Z  N  I  U  F  E  O  C  R
T  W  T  C  O  U  A  K  U  R  Q  O  D  V  A  T  H  O  B  O
E  O  R  Y  Z  T  T  R  I  R  D  L  I  I  B  R  M  U  U  T
G  G  K  P  G  U  P  C  Y  O  U  S  Z  U  Q  P  V  Y  U  P
O  F  U  N  Z  I  E  A  N  O  U  A  Y  O  S  F  Z  A  K  A
S  R  U  D  T  R  M  A  R  R  N  Y  S  O  M  V  L  R  S  R
A  B  C  G  A  Y  R  O  U  O  K  Y  G  O  X  N  B  R  U  I
U  P  D  T  Q  E  Z  A  L  T  D  N  X  R  L  D  B  Y  R  C
R  B  O  L  T  K  S  M  X  O  A  N  R  Q  J  Y  V  K  U  O
U  P  R  P  A  O  O  L  C  T  C  I  I  O  Y  R  K  Y  A  L
S  B  E  P  T  J  D  C  H  Z  Y  H  P  G  X  B  M  N  S  E
D  X  E  R  S  U  R  U  A  S  O  N  N  A  R  Y  T  Y  A  V
E  E  P  X  G  W  S  C  A  R  N  O  T  A  U  R  U  S  S  R
X  A  S  U  M  I  M  I  L  L  A  G  D  B  A  M  H  F  O  F
V  L  S  K  R  U  I  N  D  O  M  I  N  U  S  R  E  X  M  V
```

- ANKYLOSAURUS
- APATOSAURUS
- BARYONYX
- CARNOTAURUS
- COMPSOGNATHUS
- GALLIMIMUS
- INDOMINUS REX
- INDORAPTOR
- MOSASAURUS
- PTERANODON
- STYGIMOLOCH
- STEGOSAURUS
- TRICERATOPS
- TYRANNOSAURUS REX
- VELOCIRAPTOR

Scientists study the fossils of dinosaurs to find out things about their physiology, diet and even their behaviour. These fossils have been found all over the world – here are the origins of a few favourites.

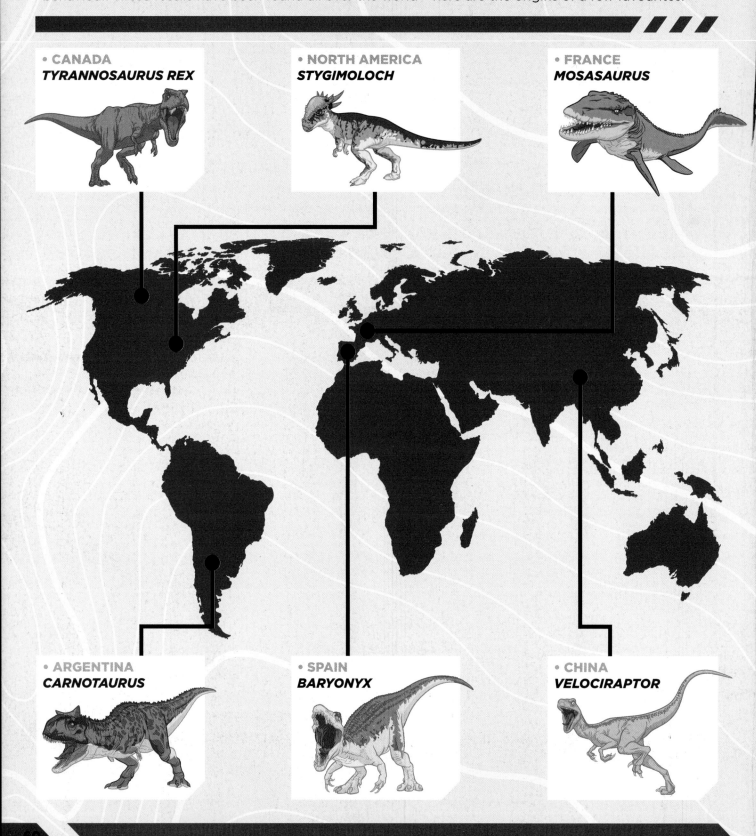

• CANADA
TYRANNOSAURUS REX

• NORTH AMERICA
STYGIMOLOCH

• FRANCE
MOSASAURUS

• ARGENTINA
CARNOTAURUS

• SPAIN
BARYONYX

• CHINA
VELOCIRAPTOR

CLOSE CALL

The dinosaurs are out! Can you figure out which species each of these pieces belongs to?

1

2

3

4

- ANKYLOSAURUS
- APATOSAURUS
- INDOMINUS REX
- MOSASAURUS
- PTERANODON
- STYGIMOLOCH
- T. REX
- STEGOSAURUS

5

6

7

8

Dinosaurs existed a long time ago during a period known as the Mesozoic Era. The Mesozoic Era was so long – almost 200 million years! – that it was divided into three smaller periods called Triassic, Jurassic and Cretaceous.

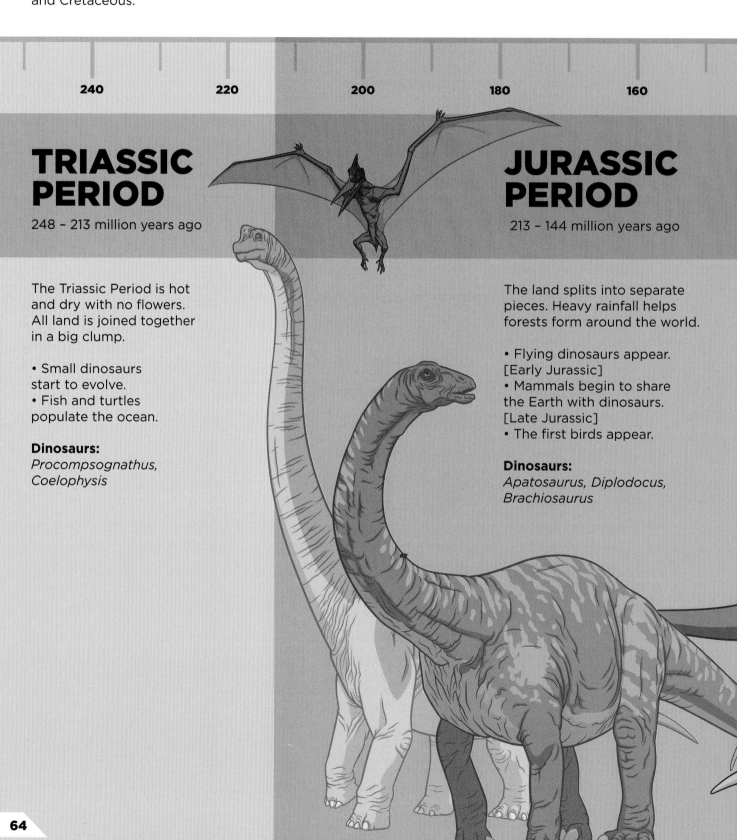

| 240 | 220 | 200 | 180 | 160 |

TRIASSIC PERIOD

248 – 213 million years ago

The Triassic Period is hot and dry with no flowers. All land is joined together in a big clump.

• Small dinosaurs start to evolve.
• Fish and turtles populate the ocean.

Dinosaurs:
Procompsognathus, Coelophysis

JURASSIC PERIOD

213 – 144 million years ago

The land splits into separate pieces. Heavy rainfall helps forests form around the world.

• Flying dinosaurs appear. [Early Jurassic]
• Mammals begin to share the Earth with dinosaurs. [Late Jurassic]
• The first birds appear.

Dinosaurs:
Apatosaurus, Diplodocus, Brachiosaurus

120 100 80 60 40

CRETACEOUS PERIOD

144 – 65 million years ago

EXTINCTION

65 million years ago

The weather cools and the oceans expand. The land begins to break into continents.

• Herbivorous dinosaurs grow armour as protection from carnivores.
• The first snakes appear.

Dinosaurs:
T. rex, Triceratops, Baryonyx

A meteor hits Earth and wipes out the dinosaurs.

QUIZ

Get to know your dinosaur history...

1. What is the name of Owen's favourite Raptor?

....

2. Which dinosaur-saving organisation did Claire Dearing found and run?

....

3. How fast can Dr Wu's *Tyrannosaurus rex* clone run?
A) 20 miles per hour
B) 5 miles per hour
C) 32 miles per hour

....

4. A DNA sample from the *Indominus rex* was used to create which terrifying new hybrid?

....

5. Which dinosaur has a tough skull made for ramming?

....

6. Does a carnivore eat meat or plants?

....

7. In which part of the Jurassic World Park did the *Mosasaurus* live?

....

8. The *Velociraptor* was originally found in which country?
A) China
B) Germany
C) North America

....

9. Which dinosaur's tail is also a deadly club?

....

10. Who is Benjamin Lockwood an old friend of?

....

11. What is the name of the island where Jurassic World was built?

....

12. Name the round vehicle used to navigate the island.

....

13. What is Zia Rodriguez's job?

....

14. Which year did Jurassic World open?
A) 2015
B) 2020
C) 2005

....

15. Which creature has a wingspan of up to 20ft?

....

Page 17:
PICTURE MIX-UP
1-A, 2-F, 3-C, 4-E, 5-B, 6-D

Page 18:
POD PROBLEM

G	J	C	P
H	K	A	E
L	F	M	B
O	D	N	I

Page 27:
BLUE OF A KIND
B and E are identical

The differences are a shorter finger, the eye colour and extra blue on tail.

Page 29:
PREHISTORIC PUZZLE

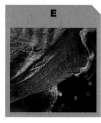

Page 31:
HIDDEN LAVA

	0		0	
1			2	2
2	●	4	●	●
2	●		●	●
			2	2

Page 33:
PTERANODON ATTACK!

Page 33:
CARNIVORE CREW

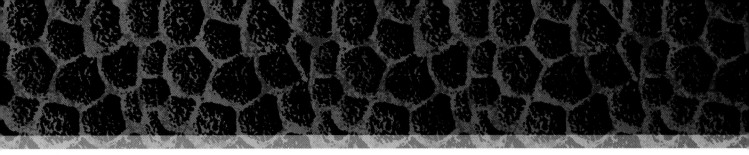

Page 37:
HERBIVORE HERD

Gallimimus

Page 49:
JURASSIC JAILBREAK

Page 58:
LAB ESCAPE

Page 59:
SEARCH AND RESCUE

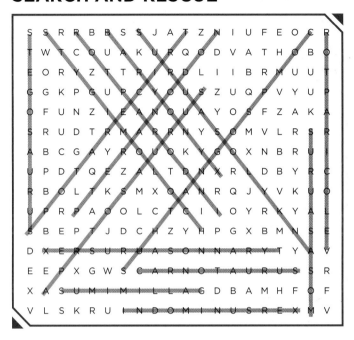

Page 63:
CLOSE CALL

1-APATOSAURUS   5-PTERANODON
2-MOSASAURUS   6-T. REX
3-INDOMINUS REX   7-ANKYLOSAURUS
4-STYGIMOLOCH   8-STEGOSAURUS

Page 66:
QUIZ

1. Blue
2. Dinosaur Protection Group
3. C) 32 mph
4. *Indoraptor*
5. Stiggy
6. Meat
7. The Jurassic World Lagoon
8. A) China
9. *Ankylosaurus*
10. John Hammond
11. Isla Nublar
12. Gyrosphere
13. She's a vet for dinosaurs
14. C) 2005
15. *Pteranodon*

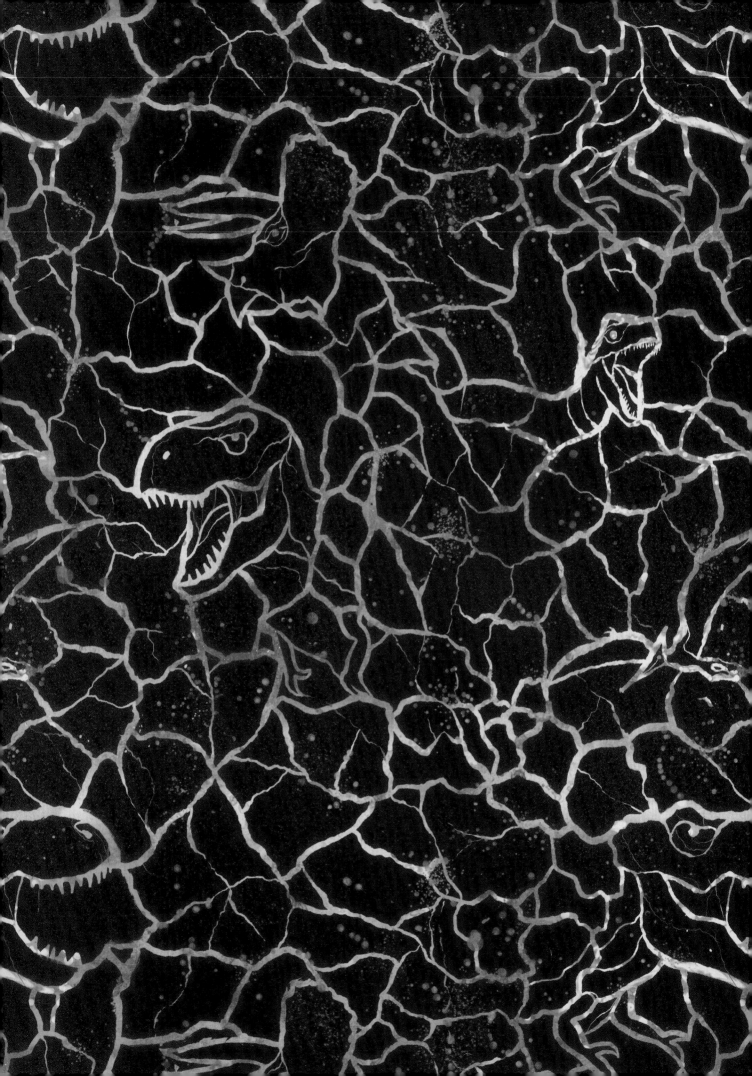